# Roald Dahl's
# Cinderella

a clock-stopping,
show-stopping
musical

by **Helen MacGregor** and **Stephen Chadwick** with
orchestral music by **Vladimir Tarnopolski**

A & C Black
in association with The Roald Dahl Foundation and Music Link International

# A slave to household grease and grime

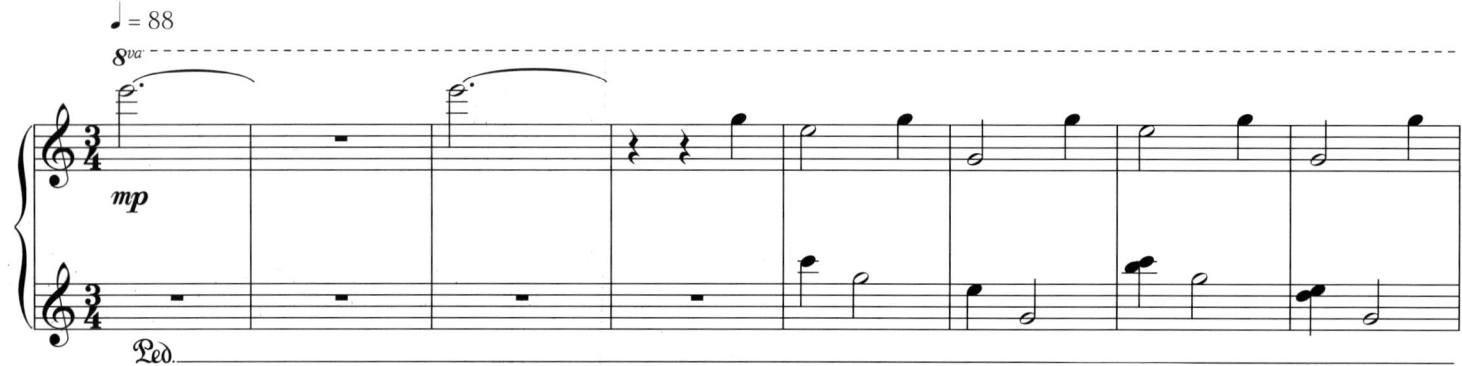

slave to house-hold grease and grime, The way she's treat-ed is      a

slave to house-hold grease and grime, The way she's treat-ed is      a

crime!

crime!

An or - phan child, no mum, no dad, Your

Your wea - ry limbs can take no more, Col -

mem - o - ries make you sad.

- lapse on the cel - lar floor.

A - dopt - ed by a laz - y lot, Who

The rats and mice brush through your hair, Ex -

lent - less la - bour ev - 'ry day,___ But Cin - ders won't get an - y pay! Tick - tock, tick -

- tock, She works a - round the clock. A slave to house - hold grease and grime, A

slave to house - hold grease and grime,___ A slave to house - hold grease and

grime, The way she's treat - ed is a crime!

| CUE: | SINGERS: |
|---|---|
| | THE UGLY SISTERS |
| | ALL |

# Off to the ball!

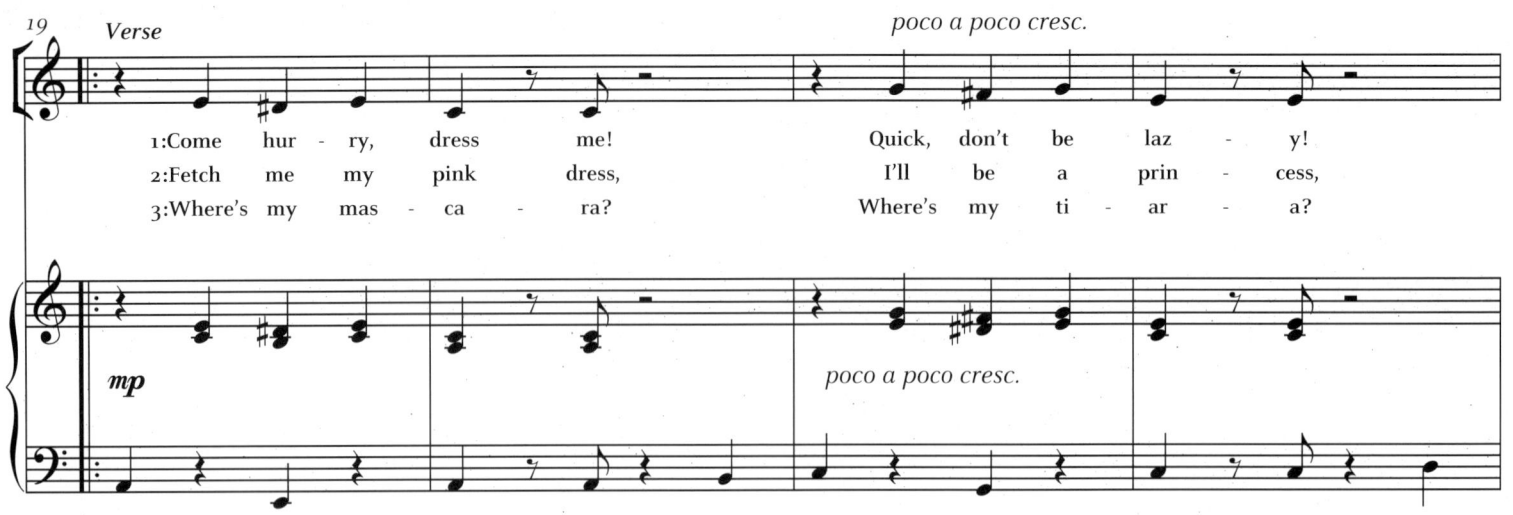

1:Come hur - ry, dress me!     Quick, don't be laz - y!
2:Fetch me my pink dress,     I'll be a prin - cess,
3:Where's my mas - ca - ra?     Where's my ti - ar - a?

Oh Cin - der - el - la, you're just too slow!
Oh Cin - der - el - la, just get it now!
Oh Cin - der - el - la, don't take all day!

We can't be too late,     We've got a hot date.
Fetch me my ball gown,     I'm go - ing up town.
You're just a ser - vant,     My needs are ur - gent,

3rd time to Coda

We're go - ing some - where that you can't go.
A scruf - fy skiv - vy, we can't al - low.
You know your place, mate, you've got to

Chorus

Off to the ball,___ de - part___ the Ug - ly Sis - ters, Off to the ball___

___ in search of wealth - y mis - ters. Slap on the make - up to hide___

___ their grue - some fea - tures, They're on the hunt___ to find a pair of rich male

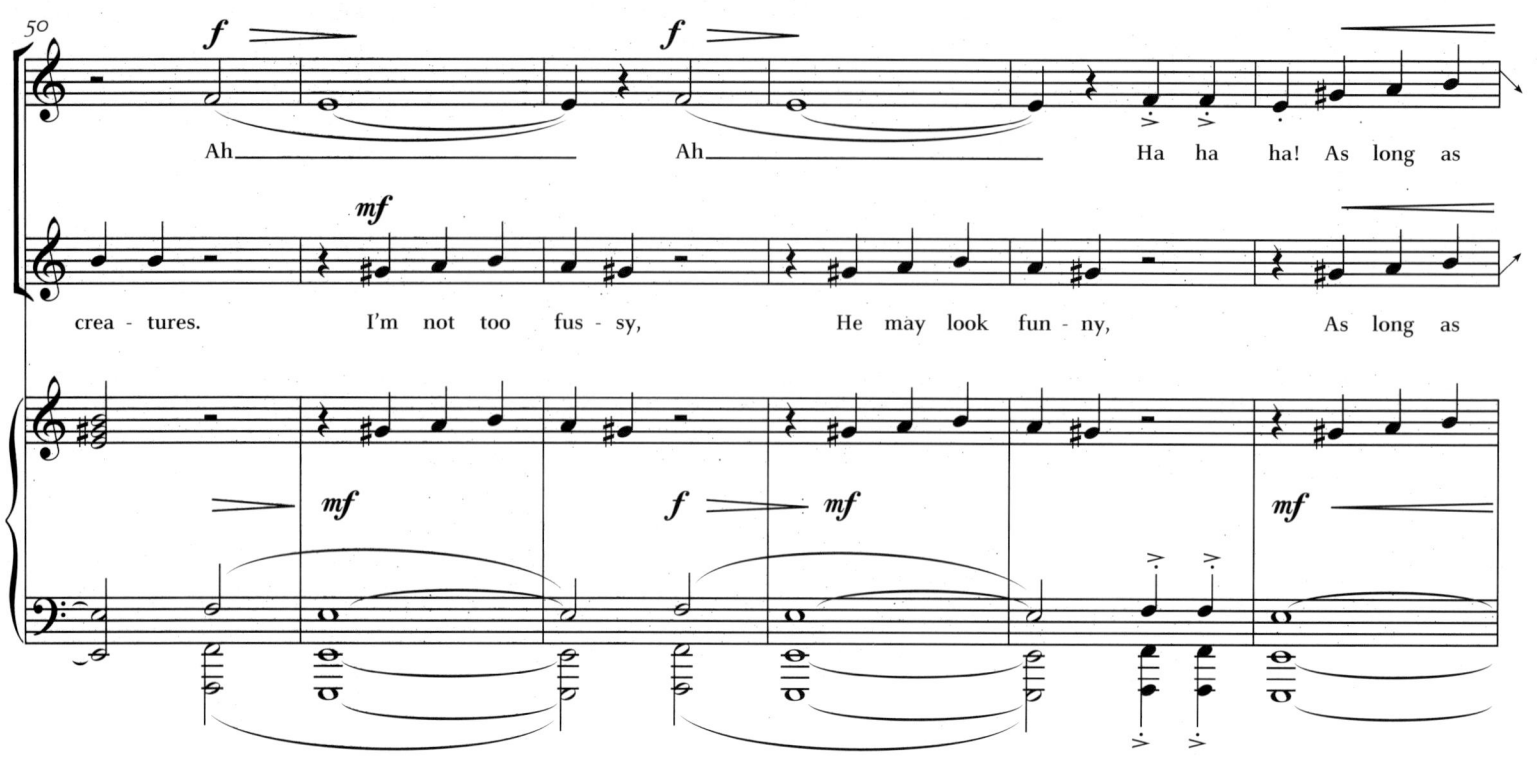

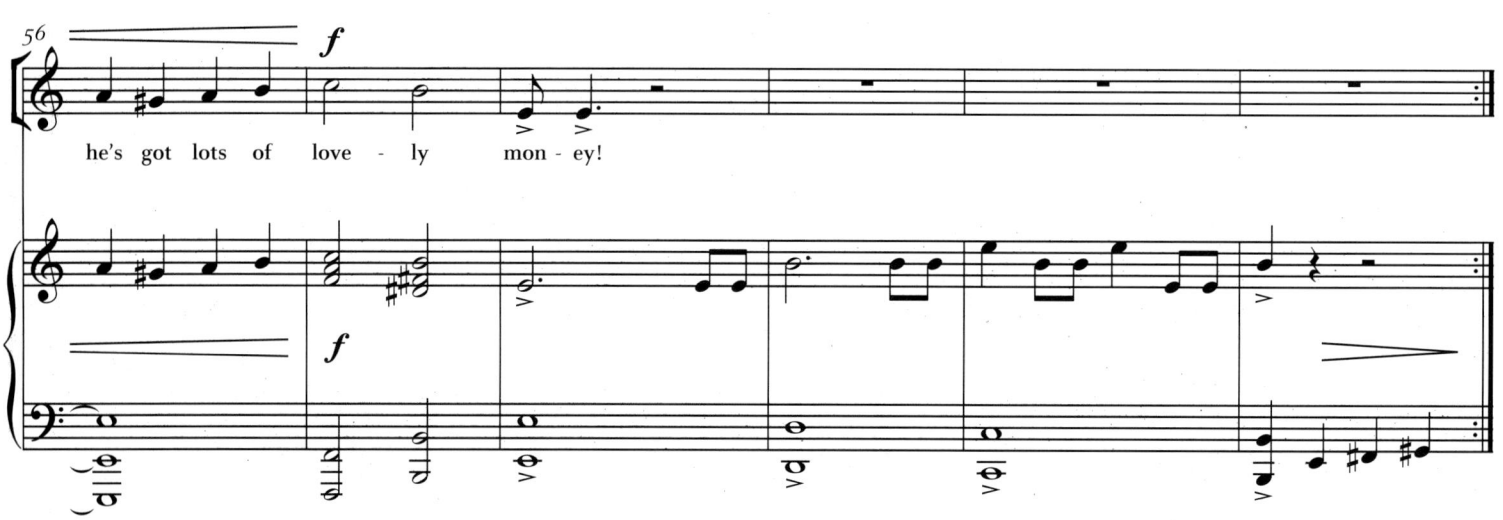

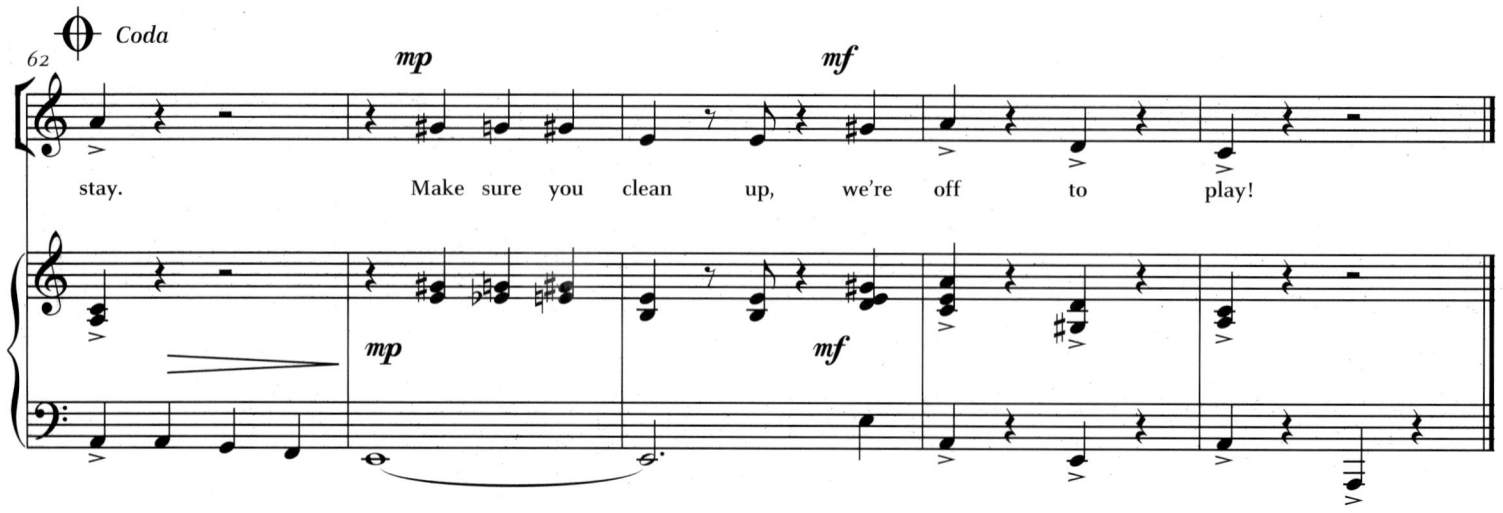

# Transformation waltz

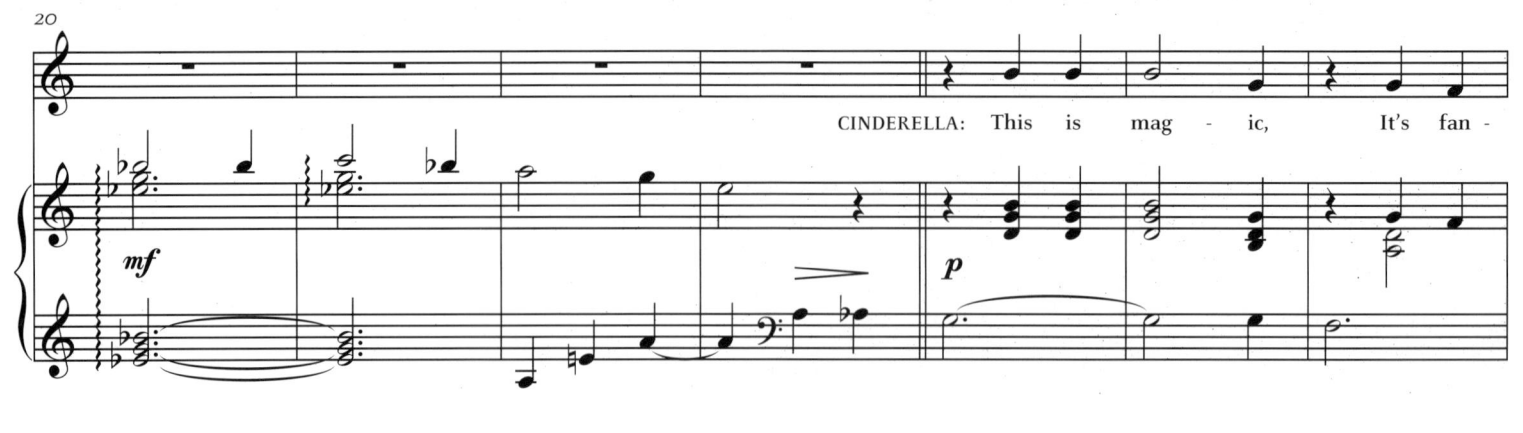

CINDERELLA: This is mag - ic, It's fan -

-tas - tic! Oh, what joy I feel. Sens - es teem - ing,

Am I dream - ing? Can this all be real?

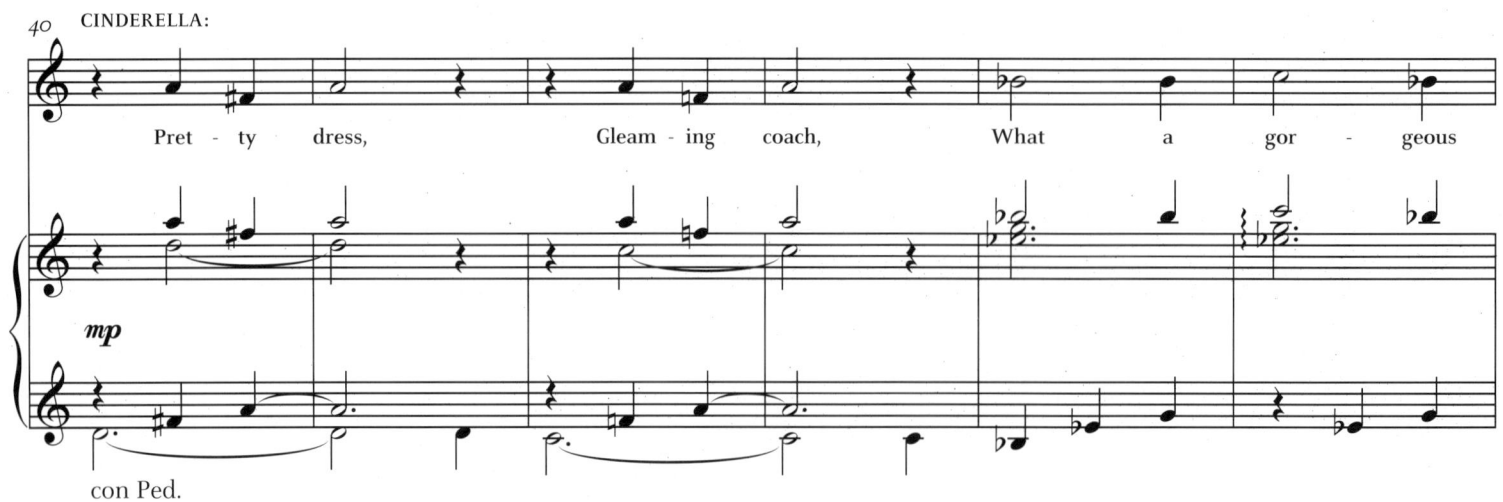

CINDERELLA:

Pret - ty dress, Gleam - ing coach, What a gor - geous

con Ped.

dia - mond brooch! Sil - ver slip - pers, two of those, I'm

MAGIC FAIRY + COACHMEN:
*poco a poco cresc.*

dressed to kill from head to toes! Done up like that we'll

*poco a poco cresc.*

guar - an - tee, The hand - some prince will fall for

**Meno mosso**

MAGIC FAIRY: *f*

thee! Re - turn by twelve and don't be late, This

*f*

*Journey section*
♩. = 84

rit.

*mf*

*mf*

mag - ic has a use - by - date!

ALL:

Trans - for -

- ma - tion, What a splen - did, beau - ti - ful sight! Trans -

- for - ma - tion, Off in a car - riage in - to the

night! Off in a car-riage in-to the night! In-to the night! And quick-ly, in no time at all, Cin-dy was at the Pal-ace Ball!

# Midnight tango

*Verse:* PART 1

Oh, pret-ty las-sie, You're ve-ry clas-sy. Ooh wah ooh, The

Prince has fal-len for you! His heart is pump-in'! His head is thump-in'! Ooh wah

ooh,                  He's  hot,  He's  all  in  a  stew.

*Chorus:* ALL

All    your    life    you've    wait - ed    For    some - one    to    come    a - long.

Per - fect    for    your    ev - 'ry    need,    Your    love    just    can't    go    wrong.    Ding

dong!

*Verse:* PART 2

Oh, hand - some prince, Aiee aiee aiee, It is her
du - ty, To be your beau - ty. Oh, hand - some
prince, Aiee aiee aiee, You give her mon - ey, She'll be your hon - ey!

*Chorus:* ALL

All your life you've wait - ed For some - one to come a - long.

Per - fect for your ev - 'ry need, Your love just can't go wrong. Ding

dong!

*Verse:* PART 2

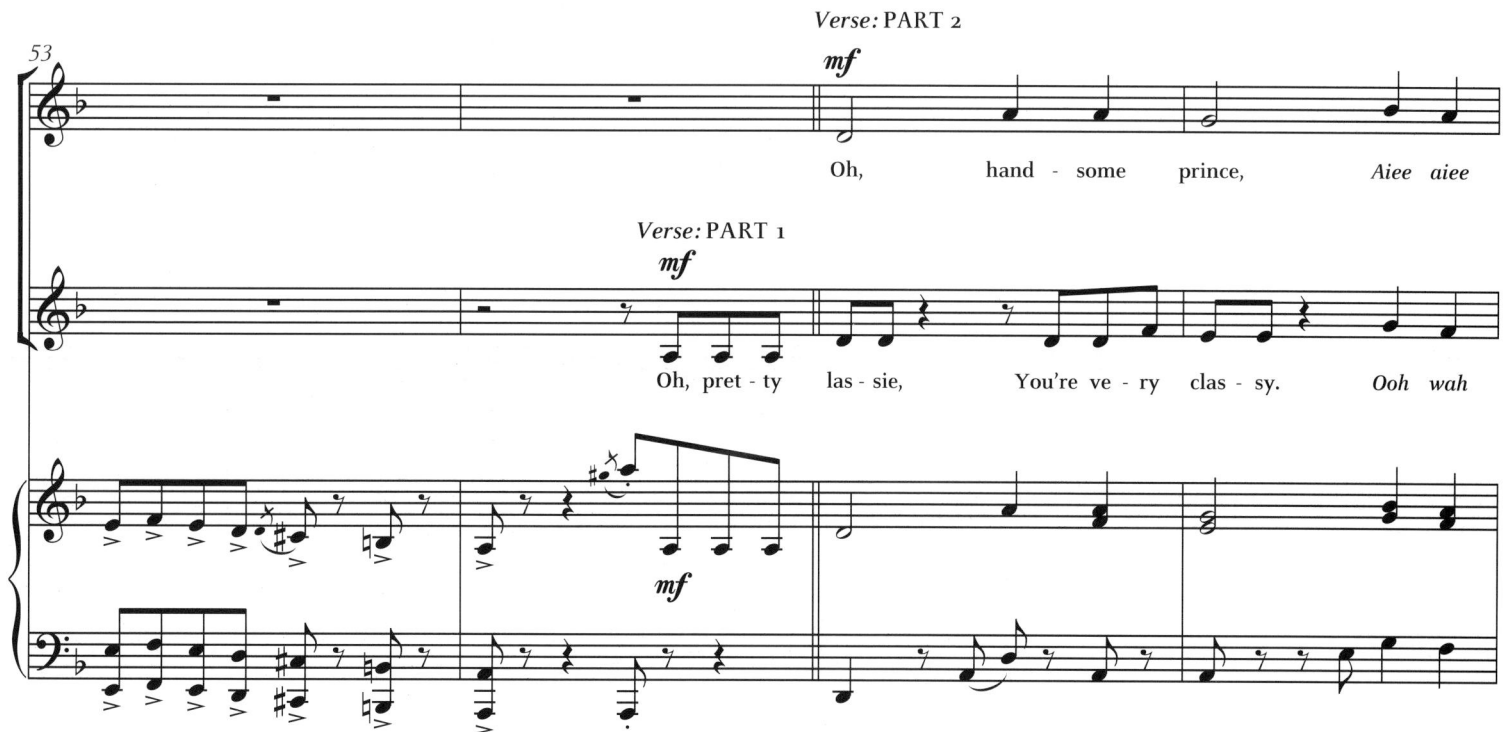

Oh, hand - some prince, *Aiee aiee*

*Verse:* PART 1

Oh, pret - ty las - sie, You're ve - ry clas - sy. *Ooh wah*

aiee,      It is her du - ty,    To be your beau - ty.      Oh,      hand - some

ooh      The Prince has fal - len    for you!    His heart is pump - in'!    His head is

prince,    *Aiee aiee aiee,*      You give her mon - ey,    She'll be your hon - ey!

thump - in'!    *Ooh wah ooh,*      He's hot,    He's all in a stew.

*Chorus:* ALL

$f$

All your   life you've wait - ed   For some - one to   come a - long.

$f$

# Roald Dahl's
# Cinderella
# Script

## Contents

A & C Black
in association with The Roald Dahl Foundation and Music Link International

# INTRODUCTION

This musical version of **Cinderella** is based on one of the poems from Roald Dahl's much-loved collection of **Revolting Rhymes**. In addition to the poem, this adaptation includes songs and opportunities for dance. There are also orchestral excerpts included on the CD; these are taken from Vladimir Tarnopolski's commissioned orchestral work, also inspired by this **Revolting Rhyme**. Various excerpts from this work can be incorporated into your performance to accompany action, mime and dance. Many of the songs in this musical also contain themes and ideas from the orchestral work.

**Cinderella** is designed to be as flexible as possible so that, whatever your resources, you can stage a successful production. Whether you are aiming for something large and impressive, or small-scale and simple, you will need a clear plan to help you get the best results. For this purpose we have provided a Production Overview (see pages 4–5).

## Who's in charge?

Professional musical theatre productions will employ a director, a musical director, a designer, a lighting designer and often a choreographer. Consider what you can do yourself and what you can delegate to others. For example, you may have some talented parents who will actively enjoy helping out with the set, costumes or props.

Involve the children in the decision making – they will enjoy being involved in the creative process and will often be most successful when presenting their own ideas. You may like to appoint children in key production roles to give them experience of the different areas that contribute to a successful theatrical performance (eg stage manager, marketing, sound and lighting, front of house etc).

## The music

The orchestral extracts included on the CD are taken from Vladimir Tarnopolski's orchestral piece, commissioned by the Roald Dahl Foundation and based on **Cinderella** from the **Revolting Rhymes**. They can be used to provide inspiration for and accompaniments to action, mime and dance.

The accompanying CD includes both backing tracks and also vocal performances of all the songs to help you in rehearsal. You will need to decide whether to use the backing tracks in performance, or whether to have live piano accompaniment, or even clarinet/saxophone and trombone (instrumental parts are provided on the CD-ROM).

If you are using the CD at any point in your performance, you will need to appoint someone reliable to be in charge of the CD player.

Listen to the CD as you read through the script and devise a plan to suit you and your specific requirements. Be prepared to be flexible – do not worry if you cannot include every suggestion, or even every song, in the show. Mix and match to suit your circumstances.

## Performing the show

There are several useful points to remember when performing a show:

- *Confident delivery and clarity*: encourage the children to project their voices, to avoid rushing the poetry, and, where possible, to face the audience when speaking and singing.

- *Understanding the text*: make sure that the children understand exactly what they are singing or saying. It may not always be obvious to them whether or not their lines are supposed to be funny.

- *Character*: often when young performers are working with poetry, they sacrifice everything to the rhythm of the rhyme. The results can be a bit lifeless and uninspired. It is more important to remember the character that is being played; most of the time the rhyme will take care of itself.

There are acting games on the CD-ROM to help develop these aspects of the performance.

## Staging and design

Nobody knows the circumstances of your particular production better than you do and you should feel free to interpret the piece in any way you feel is appropriate.

The most important consideration, particularly if there are lots of children involved, is space. Think carefully about where to hold your performance: you could perform it on a permanent stage or at the front of a hall or you might consider performing it in the round or even using a thrust (an area which, like a catwalk, juts out from the main stage into the audience). Ensure that the children can get on and off the stage easily and that there are clear routes to and from the performance area. If you are using a choir and/or piano and band, you will need space for the piano and any other players you are including. Do the children need to see the pianist for musical cues?

Where scenery is concerned, don't be afraid to appeal to the imagination of the audience. Characters can be differentiated easily by colour-coding their costumes, eg the Ugly Sisters could wear brash, garish colours, whereas the other female ball guests could be dressed in more refined pastel shades. Similarly, simple props can be highly effective, eg you could create the impression of a coach in motion by having two coachmen hold wheels made of cardboard or even twirling umbrellas. Keeping scenery to a minimum will allow scene changes to be carried out swiftly and without disturbing the dramatic flow of the show.

There are some simple staging ideas on page 6, and further suggestions on the CD-ROM. Remember these are only suggestions – you and the children will have equally valid ideas.

# CAST LIST

*All the characters can be played by either girls or boys.*

**CINDERELLA**
*When we first meet her, she is a material girl, who already knows how to behave like a princess. However, she learns her lesson when she realises her prince is not as charming as she first thought. This is a speaking and dancing part with optional solo singing.*

**UGLY SISTERS**
*This terrible pair are vain, cruel and, of course, frightfully ugly. They each have a few lines of script and if they are confident singers, there are opportunities for solos or duets in 'Off to the ball!' and in 'Off with her head!' (1 & 2).*

**THE PRINCE**
*At first glance, he is an eligible royal bachelor: handsome, charming, nimble on the dancefloor and nifty with a sword. However, it turns out that he is a terrible snob and chops off heads for fun. He has a few lines of script and if he is a confident singer, some solo lines to sing.*

**THE MAGIC FAIRY**
*Kindly, caring and good at arriving in the nick of time, the Fairy has a few lines of script and an optional solo part to sing in the song, 'Transformation waltz'.*

**THE JAM-MAKER**
*He doesn't stand out in a crowd but he has a heart of gold, a trusty wooden spoon and a special skill at making tasty preserves. One day he will make someone a loyal and loving husband, as well as lots of jam. He has one line of script to deliver.*

**NARRATORS**
*In the script, the narration has been divided up between various different characters: Cleaning Props, Rats, Ball guests and Townspeople (see below). However, these are only suggestions and you can allocate lines to suit your own production.*

**CLEANING PROPS**
*A group of children who represent the cleaning implements and products Cinderella uses to do her daily chores, eg brooms, feather dusters, buckets and mops, scrubbing brushes, dusters and polish. These can be either speaking or non-speaking parts.*

**RATS**
*The Rats can share in the narration or be non-speaking parts.*

**BALL GUESTS (LORDS AND LADIES)**
*These can either be speaking or non-speaking parts. They have the opportunity to dance both a waltz and a tango. Either as groups, or even as soloists, they could take on the singing of the song, 'Midnight tango', if desired.*

**TOWNSPEOPLE**
*They gather in the town square the day after the ball, some to try on the shoe and others to stand and gawp at the spectacle. They can take part in the movement and mime in the 'Fast shoe shuffle' and can either be speaking or non-speaking parts.*

**COURTIERS**
*Two (or more) royal courtiers are required to accompany the Prince as he takes the Ugly Sister's shoe to town: one to carry the shoe on a cushion and another to carry the royal chair. If you have more courtiers, they can marshal the queue of townspeople. They are non-speaking roles.*

**COACHMEN AND HORSES**
*The coachmen (and/or women) bring Cinderella's fine new clothes in Scene 2 and escort her to the ball. The horses pull an imaginary coach to the palace. These are non-speaking parts but the Coachmen can sing two lines together with the Magic Fairy in the 'Transformation waltz', if desired.*

**CLOCK**
*The role of the Clock is non-speaking but important. Time plays a key role in the story and the Clock can tick monotonously as Cinderella performs her chores, chime midnight at the ball and indicate the transition from night to day as the story progresses.*

**CHORUS**
*Depending on the size of your cast, the chorus can be a separate group of children or can be made up of the characters listed above. The chorus could take on all the singing in the show. Alternatively, some solo parts and duets can be taken by the actors as indicated in the script.*

**BAND OF MUSICIANS**
*There are various opportunities for the children to accompany the songs on percussion and to create their own compositions to replace the orchestral extracts on the CD – see CD-ROM Music Activities.*

3

# PRODUCTION OVERVIEW

## SCENE 1

ON STAGE: CINDERELLA

THE UGLY SISTERS

CLEANING PROPS

CLOCK

PROPS: BASKET OF CLOTHES AND ACCESSORIES

HAND MIRRORS

LARGE KEY

1-2 **MUSIC/SONG**
Cinderella awakes + A slave to household grease and grime

**SCRIPT**

3 **MUSIC/SONG**
The Ugly Sisters enter + Off to the ball!

CINDERELLA'S KITCHEN: Cinderella is slaving away, cleaning the house for her Ugly Sisters. The Ugly Sisters enter and Cinderella dresses them for the ball. When they depart, they lock Cinderella in the cellar.

## SCENE 2

ON STAGE: CINDERELLA

RATS

THE MAGIC FAIRY

COACHMEN AND HORSES

THE PRINCE

BALL GUESTS

THE UGLY SISTERS

THE JAM-MAKER

COURTIERS

CLOCK

PROPS: BALLGOWN AND ACCESSORIES

TRAY OF JAM TARTS

**SCRIPT**

4 **MUSIC**
The appearance of the Magic Fairy

**SCRIPT**

5 **SONG**
Transformation waltz

FROM THE CELLAR TO THE BALL: The Magic Fairy appears and Cinderella demands to go to the ball. The Magic Fairy grants her wish, summoning beautiful clothes for Cinderella to wear and a coach and coachmen to take her to the ball. At the ball, the Prince and Cinderella dance a waltz together.

## SCENE 3

ON STAGE: CINDERELLA

THE UGLY SISTERS

BALL GUESTS

THE PRINCE

COURTIERS

CLOCK

THE JAM-MAKER

PROPS: BEER CRATE

TRAY OF JAM TARTS

A LARGE UGLY SHOE

**SCRIPT**

6 **SONG**
Midnight tango

**SCRIPT**

7 **MUSIC**
The Prince chases Cinderella

**SCRIPT**

8/9 **MUSIC**
Flushing down the loo

**SCRIPT**

AT THE BALL: After the Prince and Cinderella have danced a romantic tango, the clock strikes midnight. Cinderella flees, chased by the Prince, and leaves her slipper behind. The Prince retrieves the slipper but carelessly leaves it lying on a crate of beer, where it is snatched by an Ugly Sister, who promptly flushes it down the loo and replaces it with a shoe of her own.

4

**SCENE 4**

THE TOWN SQUARE: The Townspeople queue to try on the shoe the Prince has found. When the first Ugly Sister tries it on, it fits and she demands to marry the Prince. Horrified, he chops off her head. When the second Ugly Sister meets the same fate, Cinderella realises the Prince's true nature. The Magic Fairy arrives in the nick of time and offers Cinderella one more wish – and this time, she wishes for a decent man. The Fairy grants her wish and Cinderella marries the Jam-maker.

ON STAGE: THE PRINCE
COURTIERS
THE UGLY SISTERS
TOWNSPEOPLE
BALL GUESTS
CINDERELLA
THE MAGIC FAIRY
THE JAM-MAKER
CLOCK

PROPS: DOORS
ROYAL CHAIR
A LARGE UGLY SHOE
CUSHION
SHOE HORN
TOY SWORD
GARLAND / CONFETTI

| Track | |
|---|---|
| | SCRIPT |
| 10 | MUSIC<br>Riding into town |
| | SCRIPT |
| 11-12 | MUSIC/SONG<br>Fast shoe shuffle +<br>The smelly feet blues |
| | SCRIPT |
| 13 | MUSIC<br>The Ugly Sister<br>chases the Prince |
| | SCRIPT |
| 14 | SONG<br>Off with her head! (1) |
| | SCRIPT |
| 15 | SONG<br>Off with her head! (2) |
| | SCRIPT |
| 16 | SONG<br>Off with her nut! |
| | SCRIPT |
| 17 | SONG<br>Transformation waltz<br>(reprise) |
| | SCRIPT |

**SCENE 5**

CINDERELLA'S KITCHEN: Cinderella's house is now filled with laughter. Cinderella and the Jam-maker are seen busily making jam together and the whole cast sings the finale.

ON STAGE: ALL

PROPS: LARGE BOWL
WOODEN SPOONS
JAM JARS

| Track | |
|---|---|
| 18/19 | SONG<br>The jam man |
| | SCRIPT |

5

# STAGING SUGGESTIONS

The performance area needs to accommodate four different locations:

**Scene 1:** Cinderella's kitchen

**Scene 2:** the cellar

**Scene 3:** the palace ballroom

**Scene 4:** the town square

**Scene 5:** Cinderella's kitchen

To keep the flow of the performance as smooth as possible, it is best to keep changes of scenery to a minimum. Using simple props that immediately conjure up a location for the audience can often be very effective.

## Scene 1

A simple double-sided backcloth painted on one side with windows could be hung on the wall at the back of the performance area to suggest Cinderella's kitchen. The children acting the parts of the Clock and Cleaning Props (see *Cast list* and *Costume ideas*) will also be on stage during this scene and will help give the impression of a kitchen interior.

Other props you may need for this scene include a basket (for the Ugly Sisters' clothes and accessories) and a large key (eg made of card), which the Ugly Sisters can use to lock Cinderella in the cellar.

## Scene 2

For this scene, the backcloth can be turned round by two of the Cleaning Props as they leave the stage at the end of Scene 1. On its reverse, the backcloth could show a dusty brick wall covered in cobwebs and spiders, to suggest the cellar. The Rats' entry will also help suggest that Cinderella is in a dank and unpleasant place.

Decide how you will show the 'blaze of light', in which the Magic Fairy enters, eg what will you use (eg a torch, spotlight) and who will be responsible for directing the beam at the appropriate moment?

Consider how you will present Cinderella's coach and any props you will need. You may not have the resources to build a wheeled coach yourself – however, children dressed as horses or coachmen could simply form the outline of an imaginary coach, into which Cinderella can step, and then make wheel movements with their arms to suggest the journey to the ball. Similarly, you could make wheels for the coachmen to carry or give them umbrellas to twirl as they travel.

## Scene 3

As Cinderella travels to the ball during the song, *Transformation waltz*, two actors can carry the backcloth (see above) off the stage, to reveal a wall, painted to resemble the inside of a royal ballroom, eg with elaborate gold-framed mirrors, candlesticks and chandeliers. You might like to add some props on stage, eg gold-painted chairs.

Alternatively, if you are performing the show in the round, you could involve the audience in this scene: they could have props under their chairs, which they then use to become part of the performance, eg plastic champagne glasses, bow-ties for boys, fans and feathers for girls. The Jam-maker can offer tarts to the audience as well as to the actors.

There are a number of extra props which you might need for this scene: an old beer crate or box, on which the Prince can carelessly leave Cinderella's slipper; a tray with jam tarts (perhaps heart-shaped), either made from painted salt dough or the real thing; and a large and hideous shoe belonging to the Ugly Sister, which could be designed and made by the children, eg from pâpier-maché or a decorated adult's shoe.

## Scene 4

To create the impression that the action has moved to the town square, some of the Townspeople could enter the main performance area, each holding a front door (eg made from card and painted) in front of them.

The children form a street by standing in two rows, stage left and right, facing the audience. If the doors are made progressively smaller in size, the perspective of a long street could be created. As the scene starts, the Prince can pass down the centre of the 'street', knocking on the doors as he passes. As the music, *Riding into town* (track 10), ends and the action moves on, the doors can step back to line the back of the stage.

As this scene involves movement and dance, the fewer props the better. However, you might like to have a royal chair on which the Prince can sit and watch the proceedings dejectedly, a cushion for the shoe and perhaps a shoe-horn. The Prince will also need a plastic or wooden toy sword.

How you stage the removal of the Ugly Sisters heads will depend on how you choose to present these characters (for suggestions see *Costume ideas* and *Extra staging notes* on the CD-ROM). If your Ugly Sisters are played by children, you may need papier-mâché heads or wigs as props.

## Scene 5

The backcloth from Scene 1 can be re-used. However, this time Cinderella and the Cleaning Props could decorate it, sticking on pictures, eg of flowers, fruit and jam jars, to suggest that the kitchen is now full of joy and busy activity.

In this scene, Cinderella and the Jam-maker are making marmalade together – you might like to have jam-making materials to set the scene, eg: a huge bowl, wooden spoons and assorted jam jars.

# COSTUME IDEAS

The story can be set in an historical or contemporary setting. (It would work well set in the 1950s or 60s, as several of the songs are in musical styles associated with the post-war era, eg the popular ballroom dances, the waltz and tango, and the vocal styles of blues and pop.)

## CINDERELLA

At the start of the musical, Cinderella should be dressed in a simple housework costume, which can be worn easily under her ballgown. A short sleeved t-shirt and leggings, tie-dyed to look dirty in grey or brown, and with a few holes and ragged edges, would be ideal. She should have bare feet.

For the ball, she will need a simple ballgown. It should be generous in size, so that it can be slipped easily over her head during the song, *Transformation waltz*. It could have Velcro fasteners at the sides so that the Prince can rip it off easily as he tries to stop her leaving the ball. Make sure the gown is not too long, so that she does not trip on the hem whilst dancing.

Whether you choose an historical or contemporary setting, a ballgown made from white or shiny silver or gold fabric will make Cinderella look glamorous. You can then add various accessories to finish off the outfit, eg bracelets, shiny hairclips or a tiara, a necklace and, of course, a pair of silver ballet-type slippers.

## THE UGLY SISTERS

For their first appearance, the Ugly Sisters need undergarments, eg vests and voluptuous petticoats. They also need simple ballroom costumes that they can put on easily whilst on stage. Their outfits can be as comically outrageous as you like, eg dresses in outlandish colours with hoop or tutu skirts and puff sleeves, feather boas, large ornate shoes and clown's wigs. Their make-up can be unnatural, eg large circles of rouge on their cheeks.

Alternatively, rather than have children dressed as the Ugly Sisters, you could design and make Ugly Sister puppets which can be held and manipulated from behind. For ideas on how to make these, see *Extra staging notes* on the CD-ROM.

 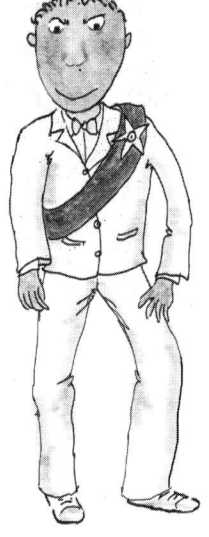

## THE PRINCE

The Prince can wear a simple white jacket and trousers. If the setting is historical, he can wear a purple sash worn diagonally from shoulder to hip and a gold brooch on his chest. For a 1950s or 1960s setting, you could dress him as Elvis in a white or silver suit with flared trousers and a pair of shades.

## THE MAGIC FAIRY

The Magic Fairy should look as other-worldly as possible. A girl could wear a pink leotard decorated with net and sequins and wear a feather boa and a tiara. A boy magician could wear a sparkly cloak over a black t-shirt and leggings. He or she will need a wand, either traditional or modern (eg a fibre optic light).

## THE JAM-MAKER

His costume should be plain and simple, eg a coloured t-shirt and trousers with an apron worn over the top. He can carry a wooden spoon in his hand and also needs a tray of jam tarts to pass around the the Ball guests in Scene 3.

## CLEANING PROPS

The Cleaning Props should ideally all wear similar, simple costumes, eg black leggings and t-shirts, so that the props they are carrying stand out. Each Cleaning Prop needs a cleaning implement to define their role, eg a broom, a bucket and mop, a duster etc.

## CLOCK

The child playing this role can be simply dressed and a clock face can be drawn on their face with face-paints. Alternatively, you could make and decorate a clock from a cardboard box, which is then worn over the head of the actor. The Clock could also have a hand chime or bell to chime the strokes of midnight.

## COACHMEN, COURTIERS AND HORSES

The Coachmen and Courtiers can be dressed in red and the horses in grey or white t-shirts.

## BALL GUESTS (LORDS AND LADIES)

The ballgowns of the female guests should not compete with the splendour of Cinderella's. They could be designed to blend in a range of complementary colours, eg pastel shades, so that the colour and fabric of Cinderella's stands out on stage. Like Cinderella, they can also wear a selection of accessories, eg bracelets, necklaces, hair slides, rings – however, make sure these are secure and don't impede movement. The male ball guests can wear black with a white bow-tie or a coloured diagonal sash.

## RATS

Colour-coordinated (eg grey, brown) leggings and t-shirts would be ideal. You can use face-paints to add whiskers, make simple headdresses with ears and create tails from tights or strips of material.

## TOWNSPEOPLE

For an historical setting, consider dresses, shawls and bonnets for Townswomen and dungarees and hats/caps for Townsmen. Townswomen could carry shopping baskets. For a modern setting, they can wear their ordinary clothes and carry shopping bags and umbrellas. Choosing similar colours for the Townspeople will help differentiate them from other characters.

# The script

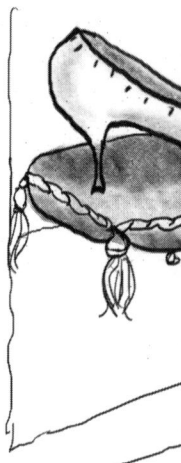

## SCENE 1 – Cinderella's kitchen

*Cinderella is curled up asleep on the floor. The Cleaning Props are in position and motionless. The Clock ticks.*

### MUSIC – Cinderella awakes

*As the music starts, Cinderella slowly awakes. Sleepily, she moves towards each of the Cleaning Props in turn, takes their cleaning implement and performs her chores rhythmically in time with the music (see CD-ROM Dance Development).*

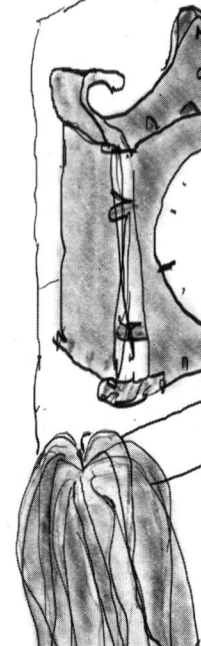

### SONG – A slave to household grease and grime

*During the choruses, Cinderella continues to perform her chores, moving more energetically as she works harder and harder to finish her housework.*

ALL

*Chorus 1*
She cleans,
She washes,
She polishes and brushes!
From dawn to dusk she's never done,
For Cinders there's no time for fun!
Tick-tock, tick-tock,
She works around the clock.
A slave to household grease and grime,
The way she's treated is a crime!

*Verse 1*
An orphan child, no mum, no dad,
Your memories make you sad.
Adopted by a lazy lot,
Who don't even care a jot!
Cinderella, what's your fate?
Is your future bleak?
Is it hopeless?
Is it lonely?
Only sadness you can see.

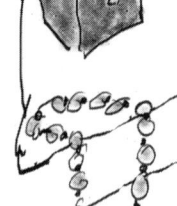

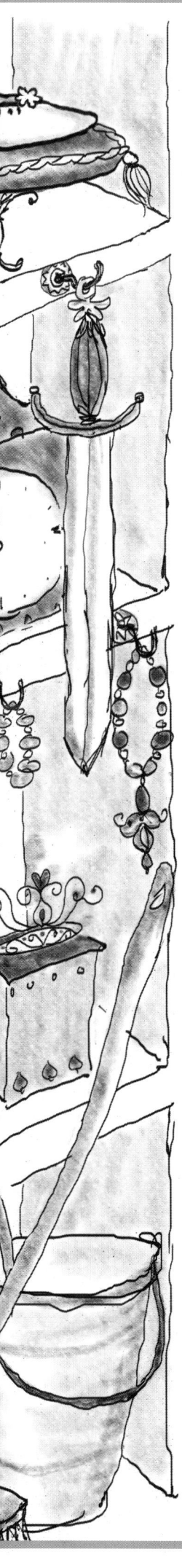

*Chorus 2*

She sweeps,
She scrubs,
She rub-a-dub-a-dubs!
No rest from all the dirt and slime,
For Cinders there's no leisure time.
Tick-tock, tick-tock,
She works around the clock.
A slave to household grease and grime,
The way she's treated is a crime!

*Verse 2*

Your weary limbs can take no more,
Collapse on the cellar floor.
The rats and mice brush through your hair,
Exhausted, you do not care.
Cinderella, close your eyes,
Go to sleep and dream.
Dream of freedom,
Dream a new life,
Free of trouble, toil or strife.

*Chorus 3*

She cooks,
She feeds,
She caters for all needs!
Relentless labour every day,
But Cinders won't get any pay!
Tick-tock, tick-tock,
She works around the clock.
A slave to household grease and grime,
A slave to household grease and grime,
A slave to household grease and grime,
The way she's treated is a crime!

Forward to
next track

*Cinderella lies down on the floor, curls up and goes back to sleep.*

CLEANING PROP 1     I guess you think you know this story.

CLEANING PROP 2     You don't. The real one's much more gory.

CLEANING PROP 1     The phoney one, the one you know,
Was cooked up years and years ago,
And made to sound all soft and sappy
Just to keep the children happy.

CLEANING PROP 2     Mind you, they got the first bit right,
The bit where, in the dead of night,
The Ugly Sisters, jewels and all,
Departed for the Palace Ball.

9

## MUSIC – The Ugly Sisters enter

*Ugly Sister 1 enters stage left and kicks or prods Cinderella to wake her. Ugly Sister 2 enters stage right. Both are dressed in their underwear.*

## SONG – Off to the ball!

*During the song, Cinderella runs back and forth, taking clothes and jewellery from a basket and helping her Ugly Sisters get dressed for the palace ball. As Cinderella works, the Ugly Sisters put on their make-up and preen and admire themselves in hand mirrors.*

*Verse 1*

UGLY SISTERS    Come hurry, dress me!
Quick, don't be lazy!
Oh Cinderella, you're just too slow!
We can't be too late,
We've got a hot date.
We're going somewhere that you can't go.

ALL
(NOT UGLY SISTERS)

*Chorus*

Off to the ball, depart the Ugly Sisters,
Off to the ball, in search of wealthy misters.
Slap on the make-up to hide their gruesome features,
They're on the hunt to find a pair of rich male creatures.

GROUP 1    Ah____

GROUP 2    I'm not too fussy,

GROUP 1    Ah____

GROUP 2    He may look funny,

GROUP 1    Ha ha ha!

ALL    As long as he's got lots of lovely money!

*Verse 2*

UGLY SISTERS    Fetch me my pink dress,
I'll be a princess,
Oh Cinderella, just get it now!
Fetch me my ball gown,
I'm going up town.
A scruffy skivvy, we can't allow.

10

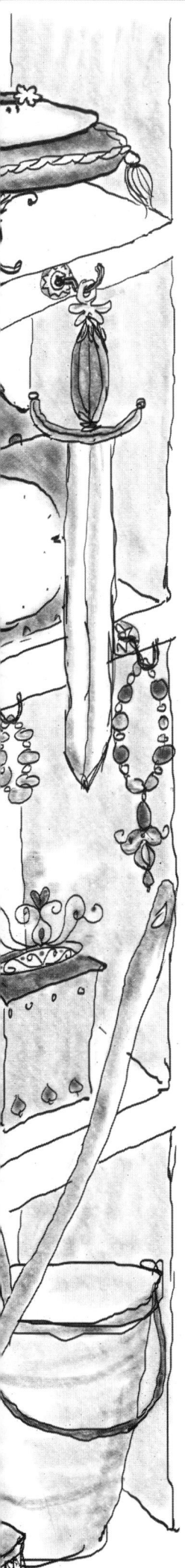

| ALL (NOT UGLY SISTERS) | *Chorus*<br>Off to the ball, depart the Ugly Sisters,<br>Off to the ball, in search of wealthy misters.<br>Slap on the make-up to hide their gruesome features,<br>They're on the hunt to find a pair of rich male creatures. |
|---|---|
| GROUP 1 | Ah____ |
| GROUP 2 | I'm not too fussy, |
| GROUP 1 | Ah____ |
| GROUP 2 | He may look funny, |
| GROUP 1 | Ha ha ha! |
| ALL | As long as he's got lots of lovely money! |

*Verse 3*

| UGLY SISTERS | Where's my mascara?<br>Where's my tiara?<br>Oh Cinderella, don't take all day!<br>You're just a servant,<br>My needs are urgent,<br>You know your place, mate, you've got to stay.<br>Make sure you clean up, we're off to play! |
|---|---|

▐▐ Forward to next track

*At the end of the song, the Ugly Sisters take a big key and escort Cinderella off stage left. The Cleaning Props exit.*

# Scene 2 - From the cellar to the ball

*The stage is empty. Cinderella enters, looking scared and sad. The Rats scuttle in.*

| RAT 1 | So darling little Cinderella<br>Was locked up in a slimy cellar, |
|---|---|
| RAT 2 | Where rats who wanted things to eat,<br>Began to nibble at her feet.<br>She bellowed |
| CINDERELLA | Help! Let me out! |

*Cinderella sits down, puts her head in her hands and sobs.*

| RAT 1 | The Magic Fairy heard her shout. |
|---|---|

11

## MUSIC – The appearance of the Magic Fairy

*The Magic Fairy enters as the music starts. She tiptoes and twirls her way through the audience, sprinkling glitter and waving a magic wand. After Rat 2 says 'in a blaze of light', a spotlight beams down upon the Magic Fairy.*

Forward to
next track

| | |
|---|---|
| RAT 2 | Appearing in a blaze of light, She said, |
| MAGIC FAIRY | My dear, are you all right? |

*The Magic Fairy bends down to comfort Cinderella who is still weeping. Cinderella is not impressed by the Fairy's appearance and has a tantrum.*

| | |
|---|---|
| CINDERELLA | *All right?* |
| RAT 3 | cried Cindy. |
| CINDERELLA | Can't you see, I feel as rotten as can be! |
| RAT 3 | She beat her fist against the wall, And shouted, |
| CINDERELLA | Get me to the Ball! There is a Disco at the Palace! The rest have gone and I am jalous! I want a dress! I want a coach! And earrings and a diamond brooch! And silver slippers, two of those! And lovely nylon pantyhose! Done up like that I'll guarantee The handsome Prince will fall for me! |
| RAT 3 | The Fairy said, |
| MAGIC FAIRY | Hang on a tick. |
| RAT 3 | She gave her wand a mighty flick... |

## SONG – Transformation waltz

*This song is in three sections:*

**Wand section**: *The Magic Fairy waves her wand during the introduction and the coachmen and horses enter. The coachmen are carrying a ballgown, jewellery and silver slippers, which they present to Cinderella. Cinderella quickly dresses herself for the ball as the Magic Fairy sings her lines.*

12

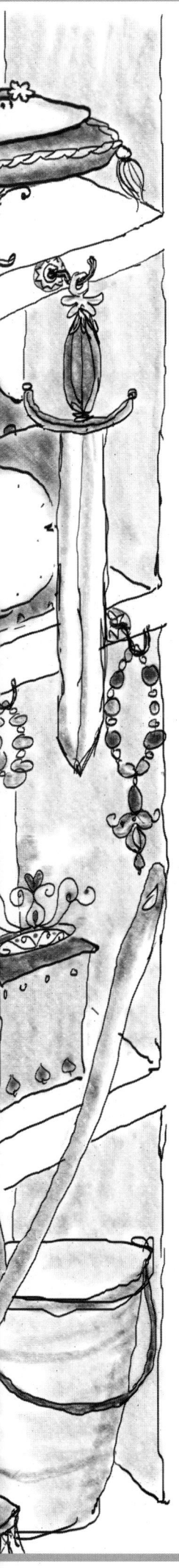

| MAGIC FAIRY | Here's your dress,<br>Here's your coach,<br>Earrings and a diamond brooch!<br>Silver slippers, two of those,<br>And lovely nylon pantyhose! |
|---|---|
| CINDERELLA | This is magic,<br>It's fantastic!<br>Oh, what joy I feel.<br>Senses teeming,<br>Am I dreaming?<br>Can this all be real?<br><br>Pretty dress,<br>Gleaming coach,<br>What a gorgeous diamond brooch!<br>Silver slippers, two of those,<br>I'm dressed to kill from head to toes! |
| MAGIC FAIRY<br>AND COACHMEN | Done up like that we'll guarantee,<br>The handsome prince will fall for thee! |
| MAGIC FAIRY | Return by twelve and don't be late,<br>This magic has a use-by-date! |

*The Magic Fairy exits.*

***Journey section**: as the words 'Off in a carriage and into the night' are sung, the Horses and Coachmen form the outline of an imaginary coach, which Cinderella steps into. The Horses mime trotting and the Coachmen make wheel movements with both arms as if transporting her to the ball.*

*When the words 'Cindy was at the Palace Ball!' are heard, the Prince, Courtiers and Ball guests enter and take their partners for the waltz. The Prince takes Cinderella as his partner. The Ugly Sisters enter, one from stage left and one from stage right. The Clock stands in a corner.*

| ALL | Transformation,<br>What a splendid, beautiful sight!<br>Transformation,<br>Off in a carriage into the night!<br>Off in a carriage into the night!<br>Into the night! *(spoken)*<br>And quickly, in no time at all,<br>Cindy was at the Palace Ball! |
|---|---|

*Waltz section (instrumental)*

*All dance the waltz. The Ugly Sisters dance in a comical uncoordinated manner either together or each on their own. The Jam-maker enters unobtrusively, carrying a tray of jam tarts, which he offers to the Ball guests. The dancers bow and curtsey as the concluding fanfare plays and when the music ends, all freeze in position.*

Forward to
next track

13

# Scene 3 – At the ball

LADY GUEST 1

It made the Ugly Sisters wince
To see her dancing with the Prince.
She held him very tight and pressed
Herself against his manly chest.

LORD GUEST 1

The Prince himself was turned to pulp,
All he could do was gasp and gulp.

## SONG – Midnight tango

*Cinderella and the Prince and the Ball guests dance the tango. (For tips on choreographing a tango, see CD-ROM Dance Development.) As the Prince and Cinderella appear to fall madly in love, the Ugly Sisters point at them angrily and look outraged.*

GROUP 1

*Part 1*
Oh, pretty lassie,
You're very classy.
Ooh wah ooh,
The Prince has fallen for you!
His heart is pumpin'!
His head is thumpin'!
Ooh wah ooh,
He's hot,
He's all in a stew.

ALL

*Chorus*
All your life you've waited
For someone to come along.
Perfect for your every need,
Your love just can't go wrong.
Ding dong!

GROUP 2

*Part 2*
Oh, handsome prince,
Aiee aiee aiee,
It is her duty,
To be your beauty.
Oh, handsome prince,
Aiee aiee aiee,
You give her money,
She'll be your honey!

14

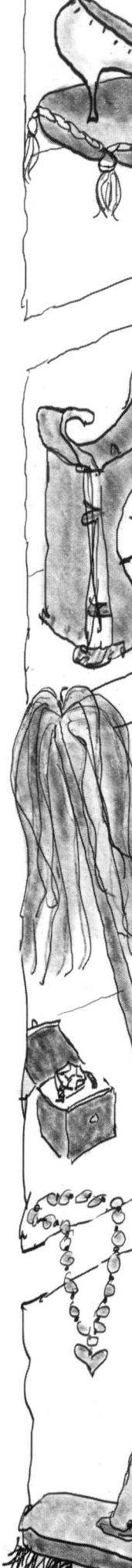

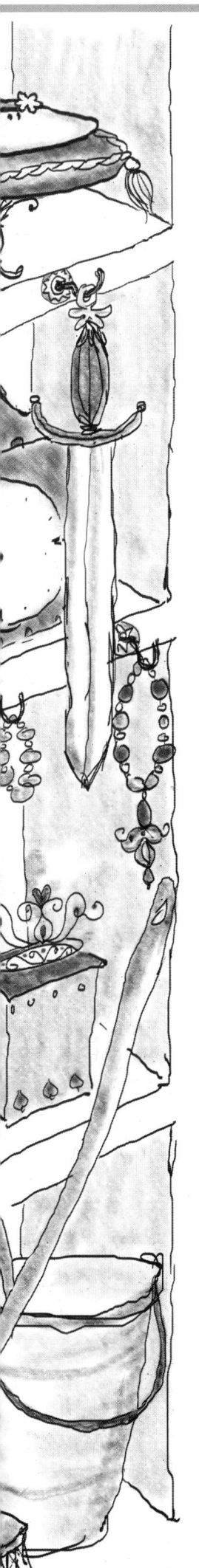

| ALL | *Chorus*<br>All your life you've waited<br>For someone to come along.<br>Perfect for your every need,<br>Your love just can't go wrong.<br>Ding dong! |

*Part 1* (GROUP 1)

Oh, pretty lassie,
You're very classy.
Ooh wah ooh,
The Prince has fallen for you!
His heart is pumpin'!
His head is thumpin'!
Ooh wah ooh,
He's hot,
He's all in a stew.

*Part 2* (GROUP 2)

Oh, handsome prince,
Aiee aiee aiee,
It is her duty,
To be your beauty.
Oh, handsome prince,
Aiee aiee aiee,
You give her money,
She'll be your honey!

*Chorus*

All your life you've waited
For someone to come along.
Perfect for your every need,
Your love just can't go wrong.
Ding dong!
Ding dong!
Ding dong!

**Forward to next track**

*As the Clock strikes midnight, all freeze. The Clock can play the clock chimes on a hand chime or hand bell in time with the CD (the chimes are incorporated into the end of track 6) or with the piano accompaniment (see CD-ROM Music Activity).*

| LADY GUEST 2 | Then midnight struck. She shouted, |
| CINDERELLA | Heck!<br>I've got to run to save my neck! |

## MUSIC – The Prince chases Cinderella.

*The Prince chases Cinderella, trying to stop her from leaving. Cinderella dodges between the Ball guests with the Prince hot on her heels.*

| LORD GUEST 2 | The Prince cried, |
| PRINCE | No! Alas! Alack! |
| LADY GUEST 2 | He grabbed her dress to hold her back.<br>As Cindy shouted, |
| CINDERELLA | Let me go! |

**Fade and forward to next track**

15

*The Prince pulls Cinderella's dress from her (see Costume ideas on page 7) as she finally escapes, leaving one slipper behind.*

| | |
|---|---|
| LADY GUEST 2 | The dress was ripped from head to toe. |
| LORD GUEST 2 | She ran out in her underwear, And lost one slipper on the stair. |
| LADY GUEST 3 | The Prince was on it like a dart, He pressed it to his pounding heart, |
| PRINCE | The girl this slipper fits, |
| LADY GUEST 3 | He cried, |
| PRINCE | Tomorrow morn shall be my bride! I'll visit every house in town Until I've tracked the maiden down! |

## MUSIC – Flushing down the loo

*Before the music starts, the Prince places the slipper on the crate of beer. During the music, Ugly Sister 1 creeps up, grabs the shoe from the crate and tiptoes off stage. (Note that the following six lines can be spoken over track 8, which ends with a loo flush sound effect.) (Track 9 is a loo flush sound effect, which can be used as an alternative to track 8.)*

| | |
|---|---|
| LORD GUEST 3 | Then rather carelessly, I fear, He placed it on a crate of beer. |
| LADY GUEST 1 | At once, one of the Ugly Sisters, |
| LORD GUEST 1 | (The one whose face was blotched with blisters) |
| LADY GUEST 2 | Sneaked up and grabbed the dainty shoe, And quickly flushed it down the loo. |

**Forward to next track**

*A loo flush is heard.*

*Ugly Sister 1 reenters, wearing only one shoe and holding her own huge ugly shoe, which she then places on the crate.*

| | |
|---|---|
| LADY GUEST 2 | Then in its place she calmly put The slipper from her own left foot. |
| LORD GUEST 2 | Ah-ha, you see, the plot grows thicker, And Cindy's luck starts looking sicker. |

*All exit.*

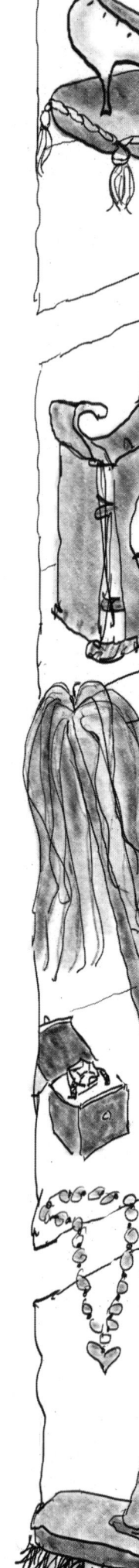

16

# Scene 4 - The town square

*Townsman 1 enters.*

TOWNSMAN 1

Next day, the Prince went charging down
To knock on all the doors in town.

## MUSIC – Riding into town

*The Prince appears in a flurry, followed by his courtiers: one carries a chair and another ceremoniously holds a cushion on which the huge, smelly shoe is placed. Ball guests, Townspeople and the Ugly Sisters enter. The ladies form a queue, whilst the others stand and gawp. The Courtiers supervise and marshal the crowd. The Jam-maker, holding his wooden spoon, is also amongst the crowd, quietly watching from the sidelines.*

Forward to
next track

TOWNSMAN 1

In every house, the tension grew.
Who was the owner of the shoe?

TOWNSWOMAN 1

The shoe was long and very wide.

TOWNSMAN 1

(A normal foot got lost inside.)

TOWNSWOMAN 1

Also it smelled a wee bit icky.

TOWNSMAN 1

(The owner's feet were hot and sticky.)

TOWNSWOMAN 1

Thousands of eager people came
To try it on, but all in vain.

## MUSIC – Fast shoe shuffle

*Those queuing eagerly try on the shoe, one by one. This could be presented as a choreographed sequence of dance movements (see CD-ROM Dance Development). There is also an opportunity for musicians to accompany the action on percussion (see CD-ROM Music Activity).*

## SONG – The smelly feet blues

*The trying on of the shoe continues in a lacklustre fashion during the song. The Prince looks more and more dejected.*

*Verse 1*

PRINCE

I've been sitting here perched on my throne,
But now I'm beginning to groan.
I haven't got up off my seat,
'Cos I've been busy looking at feet!
I just don't have a clue,
Who lost this pretty shoe,
And now I've got the smelly feet blues.

17

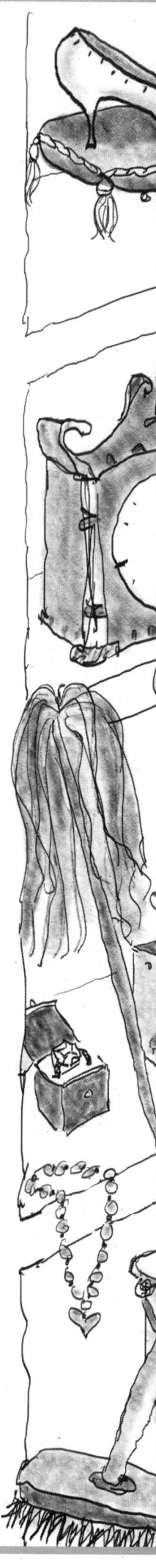

### Chorus

**ALL**

The toe won't go, the sole won't sit,
The heel's too high, 'cos the foot just doesn't fit!
The width's too wide, the length's too long,
You hobble and you wobble, 'cos for you this shoe is wrong!
Oh yeah!

### Verse 2

**PRINCE**

I've been sitting here going through hell,
I just can't stand the smell.
The sweaty cheesy ripe perfume,
Is gonna send me straight to my tomb!
I just don't have a clue,
Who lost this pretty shoe,
And now I've got the smelly feet blues.

### Chorus

**ALL**

The toe won't go, the sole won't sit,
The heel's too high, 'cos the foot just doesn't fit!
The width's too wide, the length's too long,
You hobble and you wobble, 'cos for you this shoe is wrong!
Oh yeah!

### Verse 3

**PRINCE**

I've been sitting here prodding a corn,
And wishing I'd never been born.
Verrucas, well I've seen enough,
And toe nail fungus makes me feel rough!
I just don't have a clue,
Who lost this pretty shoe,
And now I've got the smelly feet blues.
And now I've got the smelly feet blues.
And now I've got the smelly feet blues.

 Forward to next track

*Ugly Sister 1 comes up to try the shoe on.*

**TOWNSWOMAN 2**     Now came the Ugly Sisters' go.

**TOWNSMAN 2**     One tried it on. *(Ugly Sister 1 tries on the shoe. It fits!)*

**TOWNSWOMAN 2**     The Prince screamed,

**PRINCE**     No!

**TOWNSMAN 2**     But she screamed,

**UGLY SISTER 1**     Yes! It fits! Whoopee!
So now you've got to marry me!

18

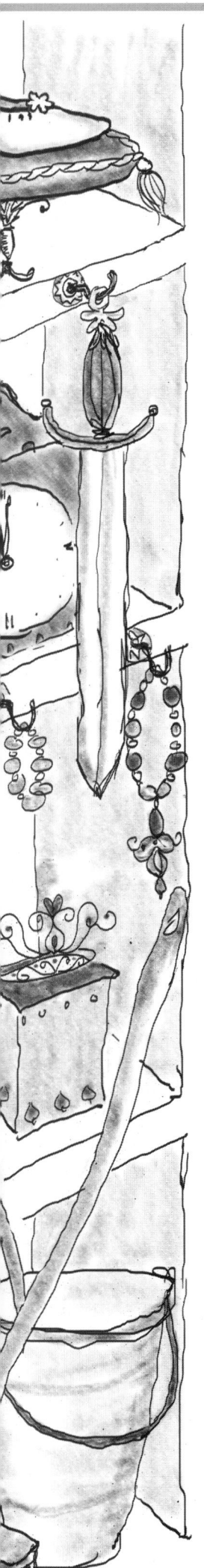

## MUSIC – The Ugly Sister chases the Prince around

*Ugly Sister 1 chases the Prince around the performance area.*

Forward to
next track

| | |
|---|---|
| TOWNSWOMAN 2 | The Prince went white from ear to ear. He muttered, |
| PRINCE | Let me out of here. |
| UGLY SISTER 1 | Oh no you don't! You made a vow! There's no way you can back out now! |

## SONG – Off with her head! (1)

*As the Prince sings the words, 'Off with her head' the third time, he moves towards a curtain or screen, draws his sword and sweeps it through the air, as though he is swiping at an object just out of sight. A Courtier enters carrying a papier-mâché head or wig.*

|  | *Verse* |
|---|---|
| UGLY SISTER 1 | This shoe, you see, fits perfectly, And now you've got to marry me. I want to be in royalty, I want to be 'Her Majesty.' Buy me a house! Buy me a ring! Just go and buy me everything! Sign on the line. Seal with a kiss. You're trapped with me in wedded bliss! |
| ALL | **SO HE SAID...** *(starting quiet and getting louder.)* |
|  | *Chorus* |
| PRINCE | **Off with her head! Off with her head!** |
| ALL | **'Off with her head!' the Prince roared back. He chopped it off with one big whack!** |
| TOWNSWOMAN 3 | This pleased the Prince. He smiled and said, |
| PRINCE | She's prettier without her head. |
| TOWNSMAN 3 | Then up came Sister Number Two, Who yelled, |
| UGLY SISTER 2 | Now *I* will try the shoe! |

Forward to
next track

19

## SONG – Off with her head! (2)

*When the Prince sings 'Try this instead!', he again moves towards a curtain or screen, draws his sword and sweeps it through the air, as though he is swiping at an object just out of sight. Another Courtier enters carrying a papier-mâché head or wig.*

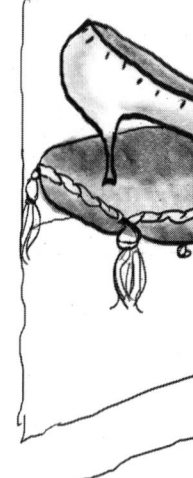

*Verse*

UGLY SISTER 2
She stole the shoe, it's mine, all mine,
My sister's guilty of the crime.
She certainly deserved to die,
And now there's only you and I.
Give me the shoe,
Make it go on.
How could you doubt that I'm the one?
Marry me quick,
Marry me now,
It's time to make your wedding vow!

ALL
SO HE SAID... *(starting quiet and getting louder.)*

*Chorus*

PRINCE
Off with her head!
Off with her head!

ALL
'Try this instead!' the Prince yelled back.
He swung his trusty sword and smack!

TOWNSWOMAN 3
Her head went crashing to the ground.
It bounced a bit and rolled around.

TOWNSMAN 3
In the kitchen, peeling spuds,
Cinderella heard the thuds
Of bouncing heads upon the floor,
And poked her own head round the door.

*Cinderella enters.*

CINDERELLA
What's all the racket?

TOWNSWOMAN 3
Cindy cried.

PRINCE
Mind your own bizz,

TOWNSMAN 3
the Prince replied.

TOWNSWOMAN 3
Poor Cindy's heart was torn to shreds.

CINDERELLA
My Prince!

TOWNSWOMAN 3
She thought.

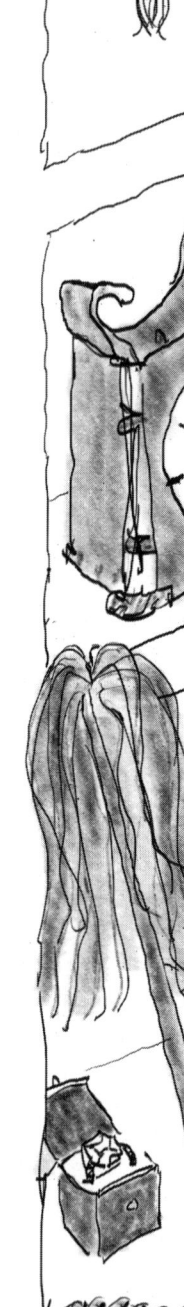

20

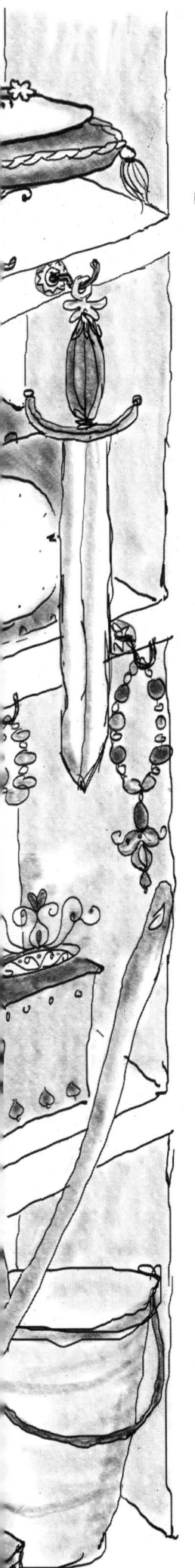

| CINDERELLA | He chops off *heads*!<br>How could I marry anyone<br>Who does that sort of thing for fun? |
|---|---|

## SONG – Off with her nut!

|  | *Verse* |
|---|---|
| CINDERELLA | I thought he was the one for me,<br>I thought he was so strong and kind.<br>But now I see a cruel man,<br>And horrid visions in my mind:<br>Shouting and screams!<br>People are dead!<br>And on the floor, a severed head!<br>Just for a joke,<br>Just for a thrill,<br>He's smiling when he makes a kill! |
| ALL | **SO HE SAID...** *(starting quiet and getting louder.)* |

|  | *Chorus* |
|---|---|
| PRINCE | **Off with her nut!**<br>**Off with her nut!** |
| ALL | **The Prince cried 'Make a nice clean cut!**<br>**Off with her nut!'** |

*The narration begins over the end of track 16. After Townsman 3 says 'in a blaze of light', a spotlight beams down on the Magic Fairy.*

| TOWNSMAN 4 | Just then, all in a blaze of light,<br>The Magic Fairy hove in sight,<br>Her Magic Wand went *swoosh* and *swish*! |
|---|---|
| MAGIC FAIRY | Cindy! |
| TOWNSWOMAN 4 | She cried, |
| MAGIC FAIRY | Come make a wish!<br>Wish anything and have no doubt<br>That I will make it come about! |
| TOWNSWOMAN 4 | Cindy answered, |
| CINDERELLA | Oh kind Fairy,<br>This time I shall be more wary. |

Forward to
next track

21

## SONG – Transformation waltz (reprise)

*During the song, Cinderella bundles the surprised Prince and his retinue off stage.*

CINDERELLA        No more princes, no more money.
                 I have had my taste of honey.
                 I am wishing for a decent man.
                 They're hard to find.
                 D'you think you can?

ALL              They're hard to find.
                 D'you think you can?

Forward to next track

*During the short instrumental ending to the song, the Magic Fairy waves her wand with a flourish. As the crowd steps back in awe, the Jam-maker steps forward out of the crowd.*

TOWNSMAN 4        Within a minute, Cinderella
                 Was married to a lovely feller,

THE JAM-MAKER     A simple jam-maker by trade,
                 Who sold good home-made marmalade.

*Cinderella and the Jam-maker hold hands as the crowd gathers round to throw confetti and place garlands over their heads.*

# Scene 5 – Cinderella's kitchen

*Cinderella's home is now transformed into a happy household. The whole cast enters for the finale. Cinderella and the Jam-maker are centre-stage.*

## SONG – The jam man

*During the introduction to the song, the Cleaning Props and other cast members perform a joyful version of Cinderella's cleaning dance from Scene 1 (see CD-ROM Dance Development). (Note that track 19 has no cleaning sound effects and can be used as an alternative to track 18, if desired).*

*During the song, the cast dance to the music, adding actions if they choose (see CD-ROM Dance Development).*

                 Verse 1
ALL              He cleans,
                 He washes,
                 He polishes and he brushes!
                 He sweeps,
                 He scrubs,
                 He rub-a-dub-a-dub-dubs!
                 But what he really likes the most,
                 Is making jam to spread on toast!

 22

| ALL | *Chorus* | |
| | GROUP 1 | GROUP 2 |
| | Cinderella | 'Cos he's the |
| | She found a fella. | Jam man, jam man, |
| | He has no money, | Lovely jam man, |
| | Just loads of honey. | Oh yeah! |
| | This sweetest love | Jam man, |
| | Will never fade, | Jam man, |
| | Because she loves his marmalade! | He makes the best jam a man can! |

*Verse 2*

ALL

He baked a tart
In the shape of a heart.
So soft and light,
She fell in love at first bite.
With him her life is so complete,
Because his jam is such a treat!

*Chorus*

| ALL | GROUP 1 | GROUP 2 |
| | Cinderella, | 'Cos he's the |
| | She found a fella. | Jam man, jam man, |
| | He has no money, | Lovely jam man, oh yeah! |
| | Just loads of honey. | Jam man, jam man, |
| | This sweetest love | He makes the best jam a man can! |
| | Will never fade, | |
| | Because she loves his marmalade! | He makes the best jam a man can! |
| | Because she loves his marmalade! | |
| | Ah oooh___ | Ah oooh___ |

*Solo section*

| CINDERELLA | | CHORUS (SECTION OF) ECHO |
| | I thought that being rich | |
| | Would bring me happiness. | Bring me happiness. |
| | But now I've found the truth, | |
| | I'm better off with less. | Better off with less. |
| | I've learned to treasure simple things, | |
| | I see the joy and goodness | I see the joy and goodness |
| | My lovely jam man brings. | My lovely jam man brings. |

*Chorus*

| ALL | GROUP 1 | GROUP 2 |
| | Cinderella, | 'Cos he's the |
| | She found a fella. | Jam man, jam man, |
| | He has no money, | Lovely jam man, oh yeah! |
| | Just loads of honey. | Jam man, |
| | This sweetest love | Jam man, |
| | Will never fade, | He makes the best jam a man can! |
| | Because she loves his marmalade! | |

23

*Final chorus*

**GROUP 1**

Cinderella,
She found a fella.
He has no money,
Just loads of honey.
This sweetest love
Will never fade,
Because she loves his
   marmalade!
His marmalade!
She loves his marmalade!

**GROUP 2**

Jam man, jam man
Lovely jam man, oh yeah!
Jam man, jam man
He makes the best jam
   a man can!
This sweetest love
Will never fade,
She loves his marmalade!

**GROUP 3**

Cinderella,
Cinderella,
Cinderella,
She loves his marmalade!
His marmalade!
She loves his marmalade!

*The cast say the final two lines of the poem in unison.*

ALL                     Their house was filled with smiles and laughter
                           And they were happy ever after.

*The cast comes forward in groups or as individuals to acknowledge the applause and take their bows.*

## THE END

24

Per - fect for your ev - 'ry need, Your love just can't go wrong. Ding

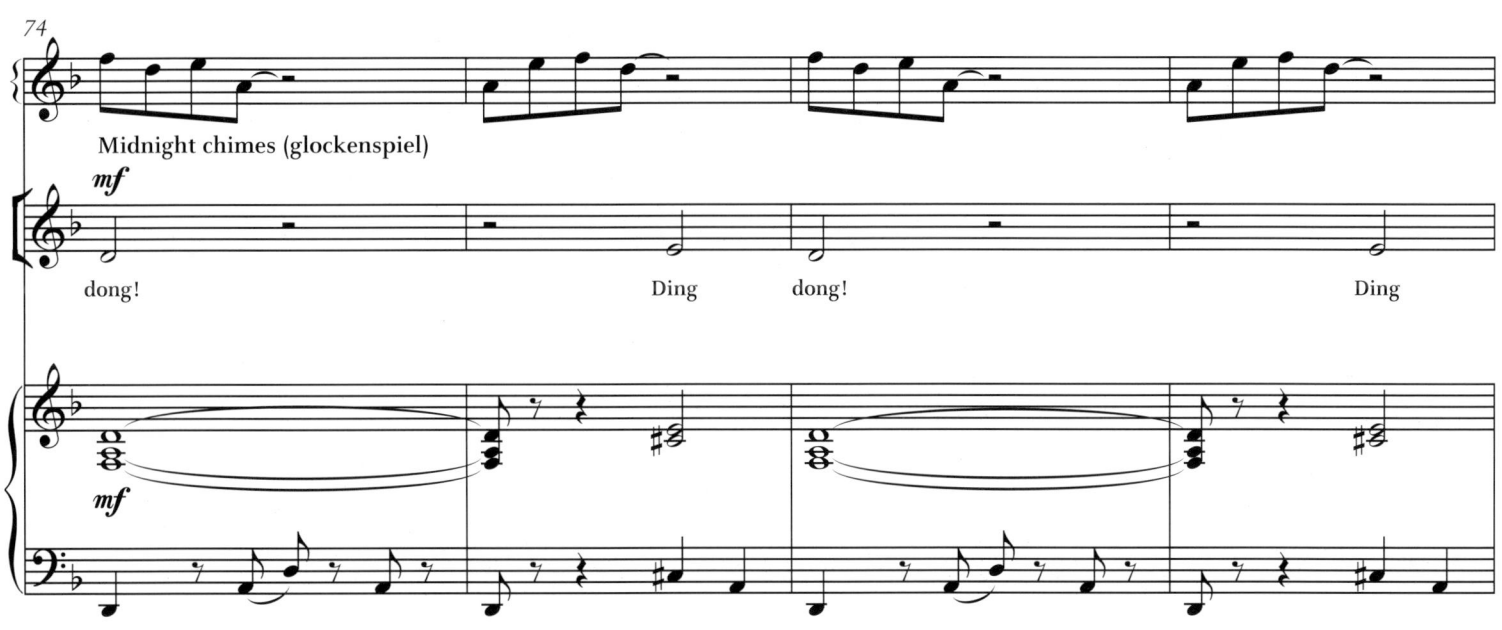

Midnight chimes (glockenspiel)

dong!                    Ding    dong!                    Ding

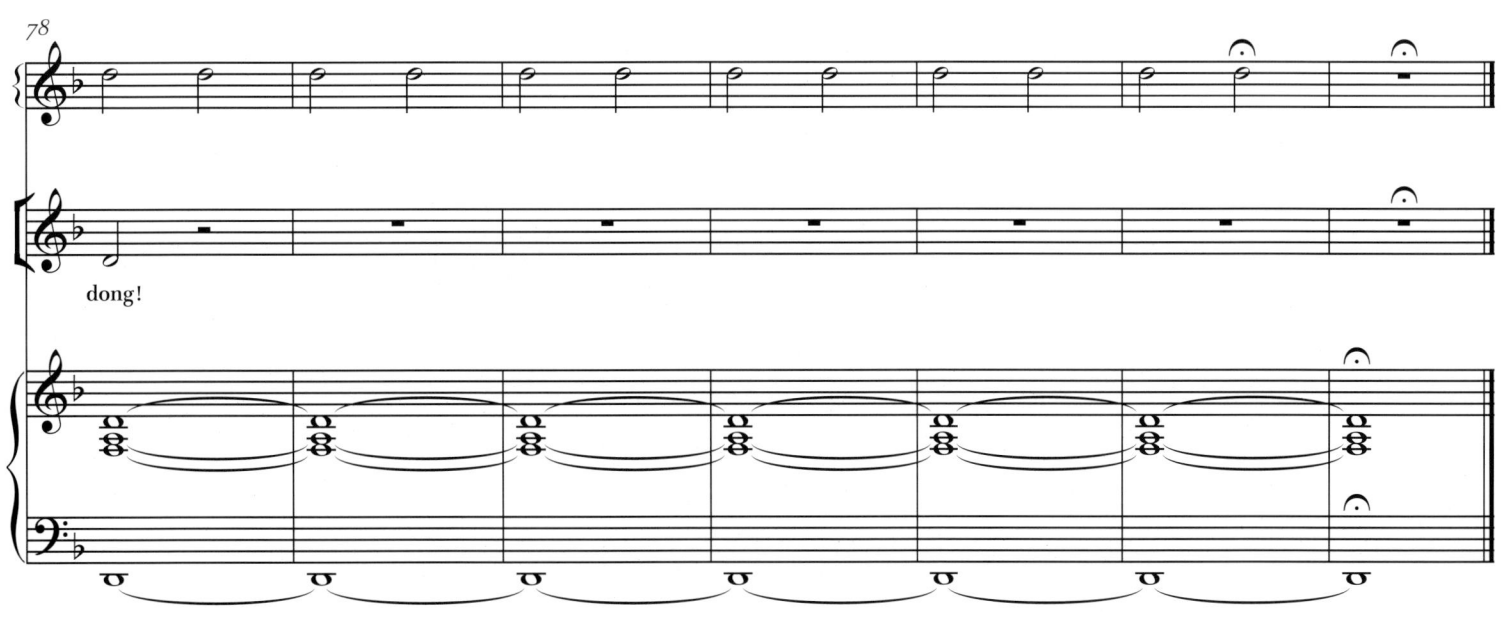

dong!

# The smelly feet blues

poco a poco rit.

molto rit.

a tempo ♩ = 100

*mp*

*mf*

1. I've been    sit - ting here perched on    my    throne,                But
(2.) sit - ting here    go - ing through hell,___               I

*mf*

*sim.*

foot just does-n't\_\_ fit!\_\_ The width's too wide, the length's too long, You

hob - ble and you wob - ble, 'cos for you this shoe is\_\_ wrong!\_ Oh\_\_ yeah!\_

*mf*

1. 2.

2. I've been 3. I've been sit - ting here prod - ding a corn,\_

And wish - ing\_\_ I'd nev - er been born.\_\_ Ver -

ru - cas, well, I've seen e - nough,\_\_\_ And toe - nail fun - gus\_\_\_ makes me feel rough!\_

\_\_\_ I just don't have a clue, Who lost this pret - ty shoe, And now I've

got the smel - ly feet blues.\_\_\_ And now I've got the smel - ly feet blues.\_\_\_

\_\_\_ And now I've got the smel - ly feet blues.\_\_\_

# Off with her head! (1 and 2)

1. This shoe, you see, fits per-fect-ly, And
2. She stole the shoe, it's mine, all mine, My

now you've got to mar-ry____ me.____ I want to be in roy-al-ty, I
sis-ter's guilt-y of the____ crime.____ She cer - tain-ly de-served to die, And

want to be 'Her Ma - jes - ty.'____ Buy me a house! Buy me a ring!_
now there's on - ly you and__ I.____ Give me the shoe! Make it go on!_

| CUE: | SINGERS: |
|---|---|
| | CINDERELLA<br>THE PRINCE<br>ALL |

# Off with her nut!

*Verse*
*mf*

I thought he was the one for me, I

thought he was so strong and kind.___ But now I see___ a cru-el man, And

hor-rid vi-sions in my___ mind:___ Shout-ing and screams! Peo-ple are dead!

And on the floor, a sev-er'd head!_ Just for a joke,_ Just for a thrill,_ He's

(SO HE SAID)  *Chorus*

smil-ing when he makes a kill! Off with her nut!

Off with her nut! The Prince cried_ 'Make a nice clean cut!

Narrator: Just then, all in a blaze of light...

*rit.*

Off with her nut!'

*dim.*

# Transformation waltz (reprise)

No more prin - ces,

no more mon - ey.  I  have  had  my  taste  of  hon - ey.

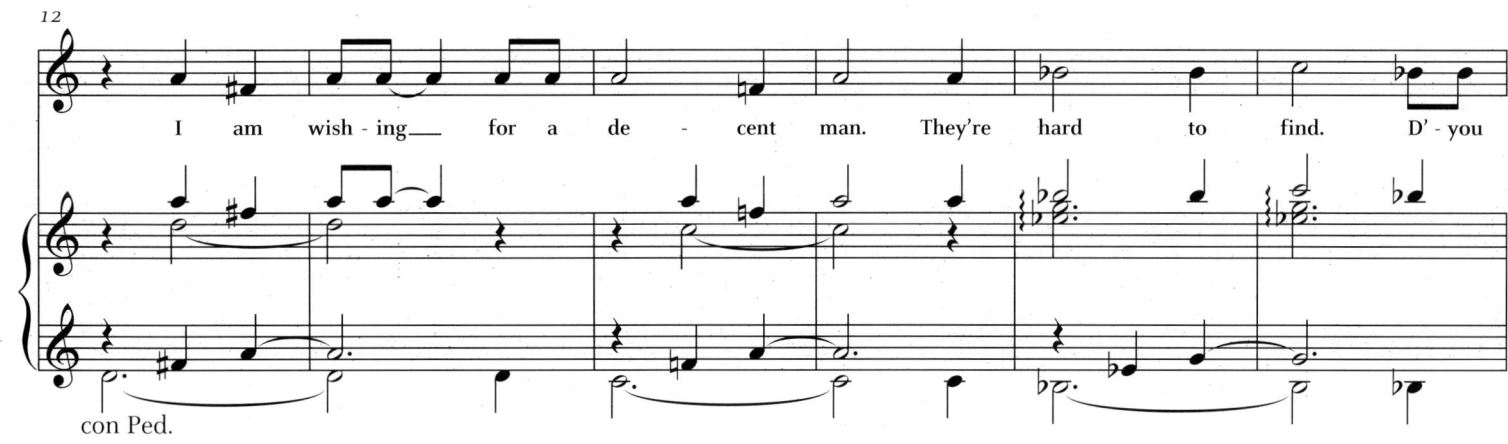

I  am  wish - ing___ for  a  de  -  cent  man.  They're  hard  to  find.  D' - you

con Ped.

31

ALL: *poco a poco cresc.*

think you can? They're hard to find. D' - you think you

*poco a poco cresc.*

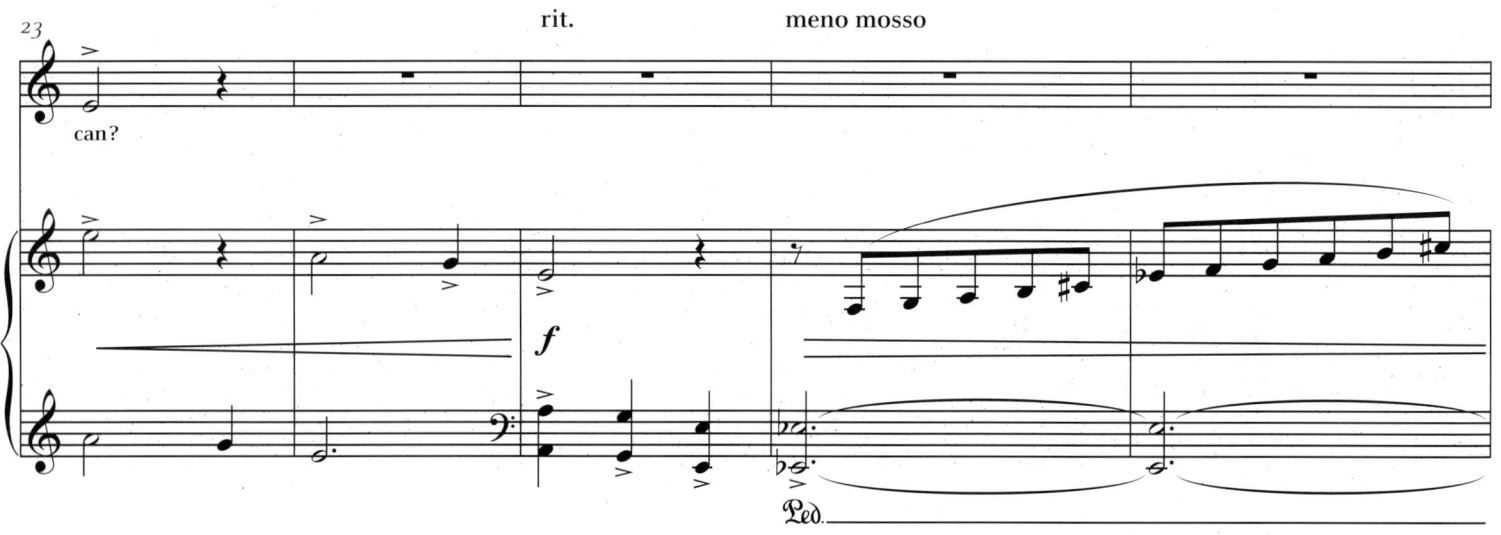

*rit.* meno mosso

can?

*f*

Ped.

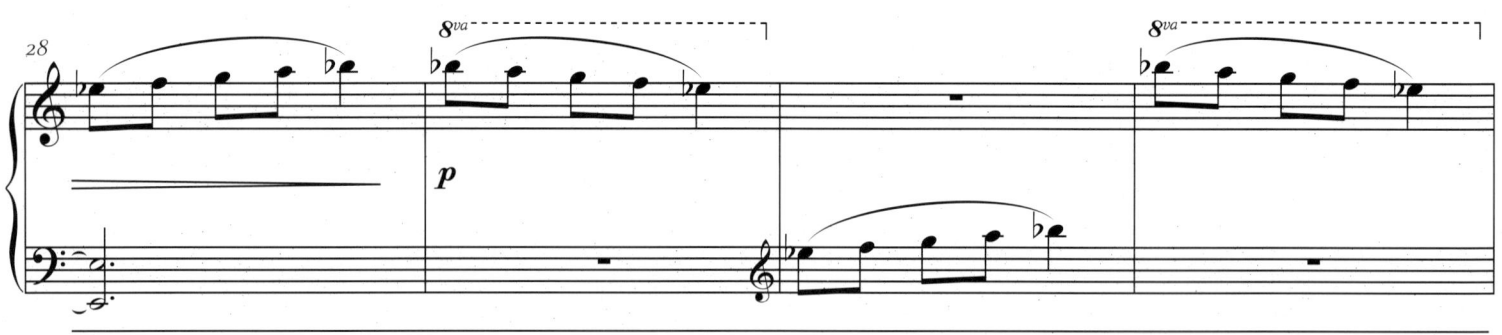

*p*

*rit.*

*pp*

# The jam man

what he real-ly likes the most,— Is mak-ing jam to spread on toast!— Cin-der-

'Cos he's the

*Chorus*

-el-la, She found a fel-la. He has no mon-ey, Just loads of

*Chorus*

Jam man,— jam man,— Love-ly jam man,—

hon-ey. This sweet-est love Will nev-er fade, Be-cause she loves_____ his mar-ma-

Oh yeah!— Jam man,— Jam man,— He makes the best_ jam a

78

el - la,_____ Cin - der - el - la,_____ She loves_____ his mar-ma-

hon - ey. This sweet-est love Will nev - er fade, Be - cause she loves_____ his mar-ma-

oh yeah!_ Jam man,_ jam man,_ He makes the best_ jam a

82

-lade! His mar-ma - lade!_____ She loves his mar-ma - lade!

-lade! His mar-ma - lade!_____ She loves his mar-ma - lade!

man can! This sweet - est love_ Will nev - er fade, She loves his mar-ma - lade!

# Applying for a performance licence at www.acblack.com/musicals

To present a public performance of one of our musicals you need a performance licence. We have created a simple and affordable system for buying licences online. Please visit www.acblack.com/musicals to apply online for a licence to perform this musical.

Here are some frequently asked questions about licensing:

## What is a public performance?
A public performance – whether admission is charged or is free – is defined as a performance to an audience which includes any of the following: parents, relatives, friends, anyone who is not a member of the educational establishment performing the work.

## What is a private performance?
If an audience is comprised solely of staff and pupils of the educational establishment performing the work, the performance is PRIVATE and you do not require a performance licence.

## What does a performance licence let me do?
The performance licence allows you to present a public performance to a paying or non-paying audience within a one year time-period (the e-mail receipt we send you will be dated). Within that time period you may present one or more performances of the work and collect box office takings to a maximum of £500.

## What am I allowed to photocopy if I have a performance licence?
A performance licence allows you to photocopy the printed script and CD-ROM text of the musical for rehearsal purposes. These copies should be destroyed after the musical for which they were licensed has been performed. A licence DOES NOT allow you to photocopy any other part of the musical. No part of any musical should be photocopied unless specifically permitted either by licence or by an exemption included in the individual musical.

## What is a photocopy licence?
If you are intending to put on a private performance of a musical and you wish to make photocopies as above for this purpose, you may purchase a photocopy licence at a reduced fee.

## What does a licence cost?
To find out the current cost of a photocopy or performance licence, please go to our website at www.acblack.com/musicals.

## What about if I wish to video or record a performance?
If your school wishes to video or record a performance, either for your own internal use or in order to sell copies to parents, you must write to us separately to obtain permission. For videos or CDs sold we will issue you with an appropriate licence on payment of a percentage fee, calculated on the retail selling price and total number of copies produced. See below for our contact details.

## What do I do if I can't pay online?
The online licensing scheme is quick and simple. We strongly urge you to use the scheme and to pay by credit/debit card if at all possible. We know that some schools may need to pay by other means, and we have a limited system for doing this. Please write to the address below, allowing one month's notice before the first performance date, and giving full contact details including telephone and email to:

The Copyright Manager,
Music Department,
A&C Black,
38 Soho Square,
London,
W1D 3HB.

## Who benefits from the proceeds of licensing?
The writers! These are the talented people who put in long hard hours and wonderful creativity to produce great shows for schools to perform. The proceeds from your licence fees and the share of the box office takings are divided amongst them.

Licence fees also benefit The Roald Dahl Foundation – see opposite for information about the Foundation's work.

# Acknowledgements

First published 2008
by A&C Black Publishers Ltd
38 Soho Square, London, W1D 3HB.
© 2008 A&C Black Publishers Ltd
ISBN: 978 0713 8195 6

Text of The Three Little Pigs © 1982 Roald Dahl Nominee Ltd, reproduced by kind permission of Jonathan Cape & Puffin Books, and Alfred A. Knopf Inc.

Original songs, lyrics and musical arrangements for Roald Dahl's Cinderella © 2008 Stephen Chadwick

Original stage directions, music and dance activities for Roald Dahl's Cinderella © 2008 Helen MacGregor

Original orchestral music for Cinderella by Vladimir Tarnopolski © 2002 RDF Ltd, published by Peters Edition. Used with kind permission.

Original orchestral music for Cinderella performed by the London Schools Symphony Orchestra (LSSO) conducted by Peter Ash, © 2003 CYM/LSSO. The LSSO is part of the Centre for Young Musicians, Director: Stephen Dagg.

Edited by Harriet Lowe
Designed by Jocelyn Lucas and Tania Demidova
Music set by Jeanne Roberts

Inside illustrations © 2007 Moira Munro
www.moiramunro.com

Cover illustration by Quentin Blake, copyright © 1982 by Quentin Blake from Roald Dahl's Revolting Rhymes by Roald Dahl, illustrated by Quentin Blake. USA and Canada: used by permission of Alfred A. Knopf, an imprint of Random House Children's Books, a division of Random House, Inc. UK and Commonwealth: from Roald Dahl's Revolting Rhymes, published by Jonathan Cape, reprinted by permission of The Random House Group Ltd. Permission to use on the accompanying CD-ROM granted by AP Watt on behalf of Quentin Blake.

Songs performed by:
Kaz Simmons and Anthony Strong (voices), Tim Payne (clarinet/alto saxophone) and Stephen Turton (trombone)

Recorded arrangements, sound engineering and mastering by Stephen Chadwick. Vocals and live instruments recorded by Stephen Chadwick at 3D Music Ltd.

Enhanced CD post-production by Ian Shepherd and Karen Manning at Sound Recording Technology

Printed in Great Britain by Caligraving Ltd, Thetford, Norfolk

This book is produced using paper that is made from wood grown in managed, sustainable forests. It is natural, renewable and recyclable. The logging and manufacturing processes conform to the environmental regulations of the country of origin.

The publishers and authors would like to thank the many children, teachers and schools who helped in the preparation of Roald Dahl's Cinderella.
In particular we thank: Pat Bilbrough, Hilary Chalk and Lola Bey and the staff and children of Sir John Cass Foundation Primary School, London; Fiona McPhail and the staff and children of Queen's Road Primary School, Cheadle Hulme, Stockport; Viki Allen and the staff and children of Tollgate Junior School, Eastbourne, Sussex; and Judith Short and the staff and pupils of St Giles School, Retford, Nottinghamshire.

We are also very grateful for the enthusiasm and support given by the Roald Dahl Foundation and their representatives: Amanda Conquy, Liccy Dahl, Anthony Goff, Georgia Glover and Donald Sturrock.

The publishers would also like to thank Uchenna Ngwe, Cath Rasbash, Sheena Roberts, Barney Samson, Ana Sanderson and Jane Tetzlaff.